Peter Pan

Retold from the J. M. Barrie
original by Tania Zamorsky

Illustrated by Dan Andreasen

STERLING CHILDREN'S BOOKS
New York

STERLING CHILDREN'S BOOKS
New York

An Imprint of Sterling Publishing Co., Inc.
1166 Avenue of the Americas
New York, NY 10036

Text © 2009 by Tania Zamorsky
Illustrations © 2009 by Dan Andreasen

ISBN 978-1-4027-5421-0

Library of Congress Cataloging-in-Publication Data

Zamorsky, Tania.
 Peter Pan / retold from the J. M. Barrie original ; abridged by Tania Zamorsky ; illustrated by
Dan Andreasen ; afterword by Arthur Pober.
  p. cm. — (Classic starts)
 Summary: An abridged retelling of the adventures of the three Darling children in
Never-Never Land with Peter Pan, the boy who would not grow up.
 ISBN-13: 978-1-4027-5421-0
 ISBN-10: 1-4027-5421-3
 [1. Fantasy.] I. Andreasen, Dan, ill. II. Barrie, J. M. (James Matthew), 1860–1937. Peter Pan.
III. Title.
 PZ7.Z25457Pe 2009
 [Fic]—dc22

                                                                          2008001799

Distributed in Canada by Sterling Publishing Co., Inc.
c/o Canadian Manda Group, 664 Annette Street
Toronto, Ontario, Canada M6S 2C8
Distributed in the United Kingdom by GMC Distribution Services
Castle Place, 166 High Street, Lewes, East Sussex, England BN7 1XU
Distributed in Australia by NewSouth Books
45 Beach Street, Coogee, NSW 2034, Australia

For information about custom editions, special sales, and premium and corporate purchases,
please contact Sterling Special Sales at 800-805-5489 or specialsales@sterlingpublishing.com.

Manufactured in the United States of America

Lot#:
26 28 30 29 27 25
06/17

www.sterlingpublishing.com

CONTENTS

CHAPTER 1

Famous Last Words

∽

All children grow up. All except one.

Wendy learned this when she was playing in the garden one day at the age of two. She brought her mother a flower, and Mrs. Darling hugged her and said, "Oh, why can't you stay like this forever and ever?"

Before that day, Wendy didn't realize she wouldn't stay the same.

Wendy had two younger brothers, John and Michael. They were growing, too.

Mrs. Darling stayed home with the children

while Mr. Darling went to work in stocks. His stocks didn't always work for him, however, and so the family had to scrimp and save.

They still had a nanny, of course, because all the other families in the neighborhood had one, and Mr. Darling cared very much about keeping up with the neighbors. But the Darlings were poor, and so their nanny was actually just a giant Newfoundland dog named Nana.

Nana was an interesting nanny, to say the least. She didn't believe in all this newfangled talk about germs. Sometimes she would lovingly lick the children right after she licked her own foot. Mr. Darling was ashamed of Nana, and sometimes he was cold to her as a result. He shouldn't have been. She was actually quite a treasure. If the children wandered or dillydallied on their way to school, she would bump them with her big head to get them back on track. She

never once forgot John's soccer uniform, and she usually carried an umbrella in her mouth, instead of a bone, in case of rain. And it did rain quite often in England.

All in all, the Darlings were a normal, happy English family. Until, that is, the arrival of a boy named Peter Pan.

Mrs. Darling had never heard of Peter Pan until one day when she was tidying up her children's minds. Most good mothers do this after their children are asleep—as if minds are drawers and children's memories are underwear and socks that need to be neatly folded and put away.

Oh, how Mrs. Darling would wrinkle her forehead sometimes at the sweet things she found in her children's minds, wondering where on earth they had picked them up. These things, she would lay out and lovingly smooth on the bed for the children to slip on first thing in the morning. Other times, however, she found mean or ugly thoughts in her children's sleepy heads. These she would shake out and quickly hide, like something pushed under the bed.

Children's minds are a curious place. If someone could draw a map, it would be full of zigzag lines and squiggles. Eventually, however, all the lines and squiggles would lead to Neverland.

What is Neverland? you ask. It is the magical island in the middle of every child's mind. It is a place children go to mainly in their imaginations, unless of course they have an invitation and a very special guide.

Every child's Neverland is slightly different. Some are in color and others are in black and white. Some have ragged coral reefs with tiny smashed-up boats, lonely caves, and tiny huts on the beach. Others have hunchbacked little old ladies, turtles laying eggs, or gnomes who like to sew. Others still have scary first days at school, trying not to laugh at church, pop quizzes on grammar that you haven't studied for, money from the tooth fairy, and chocolate pudding.

There are no rules to what one's Neverland should be. John's Neverland had a lagoon with flamingos flying over it, while Michael, who tried hard to be like his older brother, had a flamingo with lagoons flying over it. Wendy, meanwhile, had a pet wolf and a boat.

The island doesn't appear on any map, because it never stands still. If you can find it, Neverland is a very fun place to visit during the day when it's sunny. But in the two minutes before children go to bed, it becomes scary and full of shadows. That is why night-lights were invented.

Mrs. Darling didn't know anything about Neverland. Or rather, she did, from her own childhood. But she had long since forgotten, and so was confused when she bumped into the island in her travels through her children's minds.

There were other things that confused her, too. For starters, there was the name *Peter,* which came up again and again, in bolder letters than any other word in all of her children's minds— especially Wendy's.

"Who is this Peter?" she asked her daughter. "Is he a friend of yours?"

"Well," Wendy admitted, "not always."

"You know I don't like you talking to strangers," Mrs. Darling said.

"But he isn't a stranger, Mother. Don't you remember him?"

"Why, I've never heard of him in my life!" Mrs. Darling insisted, but as soon as she said this, she knew it was not quite true. She could not remember meeting Peter, or ever knowing him—no, she was too old for that. But in the back of her mind she recalled a story about a boy who kept children company so that they would not be scared. She was sure that she had believed in him when she was Wendy's age.

"Well, anyway, even if I did remember him, by now he would be grown up, just like me," she said and tucked Wendy in for the night.

"I'm worried about this Peter person," Mrs. Darling told her husband later that evening.

"Don't be," he said. "It's probably just some nonsense put into their heads by that no-good nanny. It will all blow over, wait and see."

These are what are sometimes referred to as "famous last words."

CHAPTER 2

Now, Peter! Now!

∾

Children often find even the strangest events rather commonplace. For example, they might casually mention that when they were playing in the woods last Wednesday, they met a ghost and played tag with him on roller skates. It was in just this way that Wendy revealed something quite upsetting to her mother one morning. Mrs. Darling was tidying up the nursery where all of the young Darling children slept and discovered some leaves on the floor.

She asked Wendy about them, but Wendy merely replied, "Oh, Peter must have left those leaves."

"What do you mean?" Mrs. Darling asked nervously.

"He really is quite messy," said Wendy, who was a very tidy child. With a sigh, she explained that Peter often came to the nursery at night and sat at the foot of her bed, playing the flute.

"Sweetheart," Mrs. Darling assured her, "the front door is locked at night. No one can get in."

"He comes in through the window," Wendy insisted.

"He can't possibly. We are three stories up! Why didn't you tell me this before?" her mother cried.

"I got hungry and forgot," said Wendy, who was now feeling rather hungry again.

While Wendy went to look for a snack, Mrs. Darling stayed behind, still frowning about the leaves. The thing that scared her most was that she was fairly certain they were from a tree that did not even grow in England. She searched the room for other clues, but found none.

"You are making a fuss out of nothing at all," Mr. Darling insisted when she told him. "Now come to bed."

"I suppose you are right," Mrs. Darling said. Only he wasn't. The very next night, she tucked the children in, went downstairs to sit by the warm fire and sew, and fell asleep.

Almost immediately she started to dream. She dreamed that Neverland had drifted too close to the beach, and that a strange boy had jumped into the water and was swimming toward her children. Wendy, John, and Michael were on the shore, happily waving him in.

This might have only been a silly dream were it not for the fact that, upstairs, the window of the children's bedroom had blown open and a boy really had flown in and dropped onto the floor. With him was a little light, no bigger than a fist, that darted around the room like a mosquito.

Mrs. Darling woke with a start. She knew at once that the swimming boy was Peter Pan. She ran upstairs, threw open the door to the children's bedroom, and—sure enough—there he was.

He was wearing clothes made of leaves—the same strange kind that he had left behind the last time. But the strangest thing about him was that—although he must have been very old now, at least as old as she—he still seemed to have all of his baby teeth.

When Peter saw Mrs. Darling, he bared those pearly little teeth at her and growled.

Mrs. Darling screamed, and in a split second Nana was there. She growled, too, and lunged at Peter. He dodged her and jumped out the window.

Mrs. Darling screamed again. After all, she

didn't want the boy dead! She looked down but saw no broken body. Looking up, she saw what looked like a shooting star speeding away.

When she turned, she saw that Nana had something in her mouth. It was Peter's shadow. Nana had nipped it with her teeth right before Peter jumped, and the shadow had snapped off.

Nana wanted to hang the shadow out the window so Peter could come back and get it without bothering the children. But Mrs. Darling thought that it would look like laundry drying. Mr. Darling would be upset if the neighbors saw that.

Instead, she decided to stuff the shadow into the bottom of a drawer, hidden away like one of her children's unpleasant thoughts.

"That horrid dog," Mr. Darling said when she told him the next day what had happened. "She can't go around snapping off people's shadows left and right. Why, we'll be sued!"

Poor Nana. And poor Mr. Darling, too. He knew he was being awful and unfair, but he couldn't help it. He was frustrated and jealous— about other people doing better in the stock market, and about the children loving Nana so very much—possibly more than him. It didn't help matters that Nana had brushed up against him yesterday, getting white hair all over his coat.

"Go to the doghouse where you belong!" he yelled at her.

"George," Mrs. Darling whispered, "remember what I told you about that boy. What if he comes back and Nana's not here to guard the children?"

But Mr. Darling would not listen. He was determined to show everyone who was the master of the house. And so out Nana went.

That night, as Mrs. Darling was putting the children to bed and lighting their night-lights, they heard Nana downstairs in the yard, barking.

"She is just protesting being chained up," John said.

Wendy was wiser, however. "No, that is how Nana barks when she smells danger," she said.

Mrs. Darling shuddered. Outside, she saw a million stars, some of which seemed to her to be hovering around the house, as if trying to get in.

Oh, how she wished that she and Mr. Darling did not have to go to a dinner party tonight!

"Don't worry, Mama," Michael said. "Nothing can hurt us when our night-lights are lit, isn't that right?"

This was something Mrs. Darling had told the children in the past, so she couldn't very well take it back now. "That's right," she said soothingly. "Night-lights are the eyes a mother leaves behind at night to watch over her babies."

Besides, she told herself, she and Mr. Darling would be so close, only a few houses away. What could possibly happen?

A few minutes later, Mr. and Mrs. Darling were outside, strolling arm in arm to their dinner party. But they were being observed from above. It was the stars, spying. The old stars were glassy-eyed and bored, but the little ones were curious and full of wonder and winks.

They didn't particularly care for Peter, who liked to sneak up behind them and try to blow them out, but they were generally fond of fun — and Peter was all about fun, so they decided to help him tonight. The instant Mr. and Mrs. Darling were safely inside the neighbor's house, a commotion broke out in the heavens.

A chorus of the smallest stars in the Milky Way cried out, "Now, Peter! Now!"

CHAPTER 3

Acorn Kisses and Jealous Fairies

⌒

The night-lights were still burning when Mr. and Mrs. Darling left the house. But even a night-light gets tired sometimes. It is an awful lot of work, as you might imagine, trying to stay bright and shiny all the time.

Wendy's light went out first. It yawned and, yawns being contagious, the other two lights promptly yawned as well. Then, before any of the lights could close their mouths, all three went out from the resulting breeze.

The children's room, however, was still not

dark. A strange blinking glow came from within a water jug. Inside was a fairy, no bigger than your hand. Her name was Tinker Bell, and she was in the jug looking for Peter's shadow.

Peter appeared next. "Tink?" he called softly. "Is my shadow in that jug?"

"No," Tink replied, emerging.

When Tinker Bell spoke, it sounded like bells. It was a special fairy language that only Peter and his boys could understand.

Tink told Peter that she had just spotted his shadow in the chest of drawers.

Peter threw open the drawers, piling the clothes in a heap on the floor, and found his shadow. Grabbing it, he tried to slip it back on like a pair of pants, but it would not fit. He tried to put it on like a hat, but it jumped off his head. His shadow, it seemed, did not want him back!

Peter sat on the floor and started to cry. His cries woke Wendy, and she sat up in bed.

"Excuse me," she asked politely. "Who are you?"

"I am Peter Pan," he said. "Who are you?"

"My name is Wendy Darling. I live here."

"I live second to the right," said Peter, "and then straight on until morning."

"That's a funny address," Wendy said.

"I don't see what's so funny about it," Peter huffed, embarrassed.

"Well, what do people write on the envelope when they send you letters?" Wendy asked.

"No one sends me letters," Peter said in a low voice. Now he was not only embarrassed, but sad, too, about his lack of letters.

"When your mother gets letters?" Wendy tried weakly.

"Oh, I don't have a mother," Peter said in a normal voice. The funny address and the lack of letters had bothered him briefly, but mothers, he felt, were overrated.

For Wendy, however, a funny address, no letters, *and* no mother seemed incredibly sad.

"Oh, Peter, no wonder you were crying!" she said. She got out of bed and ran to hug him.

"I wasn't crying about not having a mother," he huffed. "I was crying because I can't get my shadow back on. Do you have any glue?"

Wendy smiled. How exactly like a boy.

"You can't glue it back on, silly. It must be sewn on. I will do it for you."

Feeling very important, Wendy got her sewing kit. Within minutes, the shadow was back where it belonged, even if it was a bit wrinkly. Wendy wondered briefly whether she should have ironed it first.

"Yippee!" Peter cried, twirling in front of the mirror. "Look at me and my handsome shadow!"

"A thank-you might be nice," Wendy suggested.

"For what?" Peter asked.

This made Wendy so mad that she got back into bed and covered her face with the blankets until Peter apologized.

"I'll forgive you if you give me a kiss," Wendy said, turning her cheek to him. She was of the age when she was starting to think about kisses.

Peter hesitated, confused. Finally, he dropped an acorn button into her hand. Realizing that Peter was not quite that age yet, and not wanting to embarrass him, Wendy politely thanked him and said that she would wear his kiss on a string around her neck.

"How old are you?" she asked.

"I don't know," Peter said. "I ran away on the very day I was born, after I heard my parents talking about what I would be when I grew up."

"Why?" Wendy asked.

"I didn't want to grow up," Peter said simply. "Now I live with the lost boys and the fairies."

"Fairies?" Wendy breathed, wide-eyed. Immediately she began to ask Peter everything she could think to ask about fairies.

"You see," Peter explained, "when the very first baby laughed for the very first time, its laugh broke into a million pieces. Each piece then became a fairy."

This talk of fairies suddenly reminded Peter of Tinker Bell, who was being awfully quiet. He rose to look for her.

Wendy jumped up, excited. "Do you mean to say there is an actual fairy in this room?"

They both listened for her, but all Wendy could hear was the tinkle of bells.

"Oh, that's Tink. That's fairy language." Peter frowned. "And it seems to be coming from inside that chest of drawers."

Suddenly Peter laughed. He realized he had locked Tinker Bell in the drawer. She must have flown in when he reached for his shadow. Oh, how she screamed when he let her out.

"Tink," he said, watching her fly around the room in a fury, "such language!"

"What's she saying?" Wendy asked, watching the angry blur. "I do wish she would stand still so I could see her! Will she be my fairy?"

"Tink," Peter said. "Stand still for a second, would you? Wendy wants to see you, and for you to be her fairy."

Tinker Bell clinked something angry in reply.

"She says you are a huge ugly girl, and she can't be your fairy because she is my fairy."

"Well," Wendy huffed. "She is not very polite."

Peter had to agree.

Since Tinker Bell wasn't cooperating, Wendy turned her attention back to Peter. She had so many more questions for him.

He told her all about the lost boys, who had fallen out of their strollers when they were babies and had never been claimed.

"I'm their captain," he said.

"What fun!" Wendy replied. "But are there no girls on the island?"

"Oh, no," Peter replied. "Girls are too smart to fall out of their strollers."

"What a nice thing to say," Wendy replied, blushing.

Suddenly Wendy screamed. It felt as if someone had pulled her hair!

"That must be Tink," Peter explained. "She certainly is being naughty today!"

Tinker Bell told Peter that she would continue to misbehave so long as Peter kept being nice to Wendy. Just like Mr. Darling, it seemed that the little fairy suffered from one enormous case of jealousy.

CHAPTER 4

The Birds Leave the Nest

⤳

"Peter," Wendy said, "why did you come to the nursery?"

"To hear the story your mother was telling," Peter replied.

Wendy was a bit disappointed to learn that he had not come for her, but she asked, "Which story was it?"

"It was the story about the lady who lost her glass slipper. But I had to leave, and I missed the ending."

"That's 'Cinderella,'" Wendy said. "I can tell

you how it ends. The prince finds her, and they live happily ever after."

Peter turned to the window.

"Wait, where are you going?" Wendy asked.

"Back to Neverland to tell the other boys!" Peter replied.

"Don't go," Wendy begged. "I know lots of other stories, even better than that one."

"Well, then, come on!" he said, dragging her. "We'll fly back together. You can tell the stories to the lost boys."

"Let go of me!" Wendy cried. She was very flattered to be asked, of course, but she couldn't leave her poor mother. Besides, she couldn't fly.

"I'll teach you," Peter said.

Wendy had always wanted to learn how to fly.

"Think how much the lost boys will love you," Peter continued. "You could be a sort of mother to them. You could even tuck them in. None of them has ever been tucked in before."

This was too much for Wendy to resist. She did have very strong maternal feelings.

"What about John and Michael?" she asked. "If I leave them, they will be lost boys in a way as well."

"They can come. I'll teach them to fly, too."

At this, the boys jumped out of bed. They had been listening quietly the entire time, not letting on that they were really awake. But at the thought of flying, they could no longer stay still.

Suddenly Peter spun around. "Shhh," he said. His eyes narrowed. "Listen. Do you hear that?"

Wendy didn't hear anything.

"Exactly," Peter said. Nana, sensing his presence, had been barking since Peter had entered the nursery. Now she was oddly quiet.

"There can be only one explanation," John said. "She's broken her chain and is running up here. I want to learn how to fly, and Nana's going to ruin everything!"

"Pretend to be sleeping," Peter instructed. "Tink and I will hide."

And so it was that Liza, the family cook, saw the children resting peacefully when she entered with the very excited Nana. Liza had finally had enough of Nana's barking and thought the best way to ease the dog's mind would be to bring her upstairs and show her that the children were fine.

"I told you so!" she whispered to Nana. "They are all safe and sound. Silly dog!"

Nana was still suspicious, but Liza would have no more of it. She dragged Nana downstairs and chained her up again.

What else could Nana do? She strained and strained at her chain until it finally broke. Then she ran over to where Mr. and Mrs. Darling were dining and burst into the house, barking for help.

Even Mr. Darling realized at once that something must be seriously wrong at home. Thanking their hosts, he and Mrs. Darling rushed out. But it had been ten minutes since Nana had been in the nursery, and Peter Pan could do a lot in ten minutes.

⁓

"You simply think wonderful thoughts," Peter explained, "and they lift you up in the air."

The children tried and tried, thinking the happiest thoughts they could, but still they could not rise from their beds. Of course, Peter was not telling them the whole truth. No one can fly unless some fairy dust has been blown on them. Tinker Bell was still being uncooperative, but Peter had some dust on his hands from holding her earlier. He blew a bit on each of the children and—wouldn't you know it—they flew!

Oh, how they laughed as they sailed clumsily around their room.

"Watch out!" Michael cried as he narrowly missed crashing into his brother by the bathroom.

"Let's go outside," John said.

"I'm going to fly for one million miles!" Michael said.

Wendy frowned. It suddenly all seemed a bit too real, and risky, now that her brothers were involved.

But the sly Peter knew how to make her come along. "Did I tell you about the mermaids?" he said.

"Mermaids?" Wendy breathed. Mermaids were even more exciting than fairies.

"And pirates," Peter added.

"Let's go at once," said John.

Mr. and Mrs. Darling were almost home, but they were not close enough. From the middle of the street, they gasped as they looked up at the bedroom window. Beyond the curtain, the room was ablaze with light. Inside they could see three little shadows whirling around and around— not on the floor but, incredibly, in the air!

No, not three figures but four.

The stars, still watching from up above, called out a warning. "Peter! The grown-ups are coming back!"

There was no time to lose. Peter threw open the window. "Come on!" he cried, soaring into the night. John, Michael, and Wendy followed.

Still on the street, Mr. and Mrs. Darling and Nana watched in horror as their three little birds left the nest and were gone.

CHAPTER 5

The Long Flight

Second to the right, and then straight on until morning.

Wendy remembered what Peter had said, but it seemed that even birds carrying street maps and consulting them at windy corners couldn't have found Neverland with those directions! And so Michael and Wendy and John had no choice but to follow Peter, and to trust him completely.

He led them around in circles, flying past church spires and clock towers and any other tall object that struck his fancy. John and Michael didn't mind. They were having too much fun flying over the ocean, racing each other between waves. Wendy, however, was worried. It seemed to her that they had been flying for days now. Was the island called *Neverland* because they would never land? It certainly seemed a possibility!

She was relieved, at least, that Peter was feeding them, although his way of doing so was rather strange. He would chase birds that had food in their mouths and steal it. The birds would then steal it back. And so it went like this for a while, until someone managed to gobble the food down.

Worst of all, the children were getting incredibly sleepy. Occasionally, one of them would fall asleep while flying and drop like a heavy stone toward the cruel sea below.

It always turned out all right. Either the other children would shout, "Wake up!" or Peter would swoop down at the last minute to save the falling child, but they each came awfully close to the water a few times.

One of these days, Wendy thought, Peter might let them fall just for the fun of it, because it would be an interesting sight to see.

"Don't make him mad," Wendy whispered to John. "What would we do if he left us?"

"We would go back," John said.

"We don't know the way."

"Well, then, we would go on," said John.

"We don't know that way, either. In fact, we don't even know how to stop flying."

John thought about this. Wendy was right. Peter had never shown them how to stop.

"Well," he said, "worse comes to worst, we could always just keep going. The world is round, after all. Eventually, we would get back to our bedroom window, don't you think?"

Peter was nowhere to be found. It wasn't uncommon for him to leave them occasionally.

Easily bored and distracted, he would fly up high to talk to the stars, or down low to talk with a mermaid. He always came back, but sometimes he seemed barely to remember them, as if he had already moved on to his next adventure.

"I'm Wendy," Wendy had reminded him once when he had flown back and looked at her blankly.

"I know that," Peter had said, but she could tell he was lying.

Eventually, the children learned how to fall asleep without falling. Peter, however, found this boring, so he would cry out and wake them up anyway—just to see them jump.

At last they reached Neverland—less due to Peter's guidance, it seemed to Wendy, than through sheer luck, or perhaps because the island had been looking for them.

"There it is," Peter said.

He gestured in the direction the sun was

shining, like a hundred golden arrows pointing to the island.

"Look, there's the coral reef and the tiny hut and the cave!" cried John. "And my lagoon with the flying flamingos!"

"And there's the hunchbacked little old lady and the turtles laying their eggs and the sewing gnomes!" Michael added. "And my flamingo with the flying lagoons!"

"Hello, Wolfie," Wendy called down to her pet wolf. "Hello, boat!"

The children also saw and recognized the scary first days at school, trying not to laugh at church, the pop quizzes they hadn't studied for, the tooth fairy money, and the delicious chocolate pudding. It was all so familiar!

Peter was a little annoyed with the children for knowing so much about the island. He wanted to be the one who knew everything.

Shortly, however, the sun went down and

the children got scared. Then Peter felt better because they needed him again.

Down below, black shadows grew and strange noises could be heard. Out in the open sky, there were no night-lights or Nanas to keep a child safe. The children were on their own.

Huddling close to Peter, they flew so low now that their toes occasionally brushed the ocean. Something strange hung in the air. All of them could sense it.

"They don't want us to land," Peter said.

"Who are they?" Wendy whispered, shuddering.

Peter wouldn't say. Instead he said, "This island is full of pirates, and their captain, Hook, is the biggest pirate of all."

The boys had been excited about the pirates, but at the reality of them Michael began to cry, and even John gulped.

"Of course, Hook's not quite as big as he used

to be," Peter added, "thanks to me. During our last battle, I chopped off his right hand with my sword. Now he has an iron claw instead of fingers. If you meet him, you leave him to me, got it?"

"Yes."

"Don't say *yes.* Say *Ay, ay, sir.* Every boy who serves under me has to say that."

"Ay, ay, sir," John replied.

It occurred to John then that Tinker Bell's light might make it easier for the pirates to see them.

"Tell her to go away at once, Peter," the children cried, but he refused.

"She gets scared and lonely, too," he said.

They compromised. John would carry Tink in his hat, which he would hold in his hand. This worked for a while until John got tired and Wendy took over.

"Don't think that this changes anything between us," the still-jealous Tink clinked, if only for Peter's benefit.

Suddenly the quiet black sky was split in two by a loud boom. The noise echoed through the dark mountains.

"It's their cannon!" John cried. "The pirates have fired it at us! Is anyone shot?"

"I'm not," Michael said.

But wait—where were Peter and Wendy?

The wind from the cannon fire had carried Peter far out to sea, and Wendy (and Tink) blew high up into the black sky.

Tink wasn't all bad, but fairies are so small that they only have room for one feeling at a time. When she was around Wendy, the jealousy Tink felt could barely fit.

Seeing a chance to rid herself of Wendy, Tink gestured for the girl to follow her. What else could Wendy do, all alone in the sky? She flew trustingly after the fairy to meet her fate.

CHAPTER 6

Island Come True

ᕙᕗ

As though it were a living, breathing thing, Neverland seemed to sense that Peter was almost home. Like a puppy, it strained and wiggled to meet him at the door. Whenever Peter went away, the island slowed. The fairies slept late. The wild animals nursed their babies. The pirates and the lost boys and the Indians stopped fighting wars and just called one another names instead.

With his return, however, the whole place started to rumble as if a train were coming. The lost boys set out to find Peter, the pirates started

looking for the lost boys, the Indians began looking for the pirates, and the wild animals started
looking for the Indians. All of them went around
and around the island, but at the same speed, so
they never met.

Let us take a moment to examine each group
as it passes. The first to come our way are the lost
boys. The number of lost boys varies. If someone

grows up, which is against the rules, he is kicked out. Right now, there are six. They wear bearskins and carry daggers, and they creep through the bushes like soldiers in single file.

Leading the group is Tootles. Tootles has bad luck. The biggest adventures always seem to happen whenever he steps around the corner for a snack. When he returns, he inevitably finds the boys putting on bandages after a brilliant and bloody fight. He could be bitter about it, but Tootles is the sweetest and humblest lost boy.

Next comes Nibs, the best dressed of the lost boys, followed by Slightly, who can carve whistles out of wood and dances to his own tunes. Slightly is also the most arrogant lost boy; he sticks up his nose at everyone so much that sometimes you can see right up inside.

Curly is the fourth boy. He is always getting into trouble, and he has grown accustomed to taking the blame even for things he didn't do.

Last are the twins. We will not describe them because no one can ever tell them apart, anyway.

Instead, let's move on to the pirates, close behind, on the boys' trail. They are a scary-looking bunch.

Leading their ragged group is the handsome Italian pirate Cecco, who carved his name in blood on the back of the warden of the prison from which he had escaped. Behind him is the giant, tattooed Bill Jukes, who once took six bullets before dropping the bag of gold pieces he'd been stealing.

Next are Cookson and Gentleman Starkey. Starkey is the most polite of the pirates; he always apologizes before stabbing anyone with his sword.

Then come the Irish pirate, Smee, and Noodler, followed by a few more ruffians.

Somewhere in the middle of this dark and dangerous group is James Hook, the most feared pirate of them all. His hair is styled in long, shiny black curls, framing a sternly handsome face. His eyes are deep and black and dead—unless he is plunging his hook into someone, in which case his eyes sparkle a bright and happy red.

Hook is a different breed of pirate from the rest of his crew. Except at the sight of his own blood, he is courageous. He is a master storyteller. He speaks beautifully and softly—even when he is swearing—and is never more sinister than when he is being polite.

After the pirates come the Indians. Creeping quietly like shadows, they carry tomahawks and knives. Among them is Tiger Lily, the beautiful Indian princess, whom none dare approach for fear that she will raise her hatchet to them.

Behind the Indians creep the beasts—lions, tigers, bears, and other animals. The beasts are so hungry that their tongues are hanging out.

Finally, there comes a giant crocodile. He is hungry, too, but not for just any meat. No, he has a craving for something—or, rather, someone— very specific.

The boys stop first. They are getting tired.

⁓

"I wish Peter would get home already and tell us how 'Cinderella' ends," Slightly said, out of breath.

Tootles was about to respond when the boys heard the pirates walking and singing in the distance. The lost boys had stopped, but the pirates were still coming!

Peter had trained the boys well, and they knew exactly what to do. In a flash they each ran to a nearby tree. Instead of climbing up, however, the boys went down.

The trees were hollow, each with a hole in it exactly as big as one of the boys, and all leading to the same underground cave.

Hook had heard about these tree-doors, and thought it silly that each boy had his own tree. For his purposes, however, it suited him just fine: Seven trees should be easier to find than one!

The pirates soon arrived in the clearing where the lost boys had just been. While the others fanned out to continue their search, Hook and Smee stayed behind.

"I think I spotted that Nibs boy, Captain," Smee said. "Shall I run after him? I could tickle him with my sword."

"No," Hook said. "I want them all, especially their captain, Peter Pan. He cut off my arm and threw it to a passing crocodile." His waved his iron claw in the air. "One of these days, I'm going to shake his hand with this!"

"Is that why you fear crocodiles?" Smee asked.

"Not all crocodiles," Hook replied. "Just that one. It thought my arm was so tasty that it has followed me ever since, licking its lips, just waiting to eat the rest of me. The only reason it has not caught me yet is that it swallowed a clock, which ticks inside it. I always hear the beast coming and run away!"

"One day, that clock's battery will die," Smee pointed out. "The ticking will stop."

"Ay," Hook agreed darkly, sitting down on a mushroom.

It was a strangely warm mushroom, Hook thought. Standing up, he pulled at the mushroom and discovered that its top easily came off. The headless mushroom then started to smoke. Why, it wasn't a mushroom at all; it was a chimney!

Down the chimney, Hook heard voices. It was the lost boys; he had found their cave!

Looking around now, he could also see holes in seven of the nearby trees. The entrances!

"I heard them say that Peter is away," Smee whispered.

Hook smiled and nodded. He carefully replaced the mushroom top. He had a plan.

"Let's return to the ship," Hook said. "We will bake a cake for them and leave it on Marooners' Rock in the mermaid lagoon. The boys are sure to find it and gobble it up, and it will make them sick so that we can more easily capture them."

Oh, how Hook and Smee laughed as they walked back to the boat. Soon, however, another sound replaced their laughter. It was the sound of ticking! Hook stopped short, shuddering.

"Run!" yelled Smee, but Hook was already gone.

CHAPTER 7

The Wendy Bird

⌒⌒

Unaware that the pirates had found their hiding place, the boys waited for a while and then emerged from their underground cave. Suddenly Nibs saw something in the sky.

"Look at that white bird," he said. "It sounds as if it is saying, *Poor Wendy!* It must be a Wendy bird."

It wasn't actually a bird that Nibs saw at all, but poor Wendy herself, flying up above.

Now the boys heard another sound. It was the voice of Tinker Bell, shrill and jealous. She was no longer pretending to be nice to Wendy, but was pinching her and trying to make her fall.

"Peter wants you to shoot this white bird," Tink called down to the boys.

"Quick," the boys cried. "Bows and arrows!"

Tootles excitedly fitted an arrow to his bow. "Get out of the way, Tink," he shouted. He fired, and Wendy fluttered to the ground with an arrow in her breast.

"I shot the Wendy bird!" Tootles bragged. "Peter will be so proud of me!"

"Silly donkey," Tinker Bell clinked, laughing at her trick before going to hide. She knew she would be in trouble for urging poor Tootles to shoot Wendy.

Slightly frowned as he looked at Wendy.

"That is no bird," he said. "I think it is a lady."

"A lady?" Tootles replied nervously.

"Peter was bringing a lady to take care of us, and you've gone and killed her!" Curly said.

Tootles took a deep, sad breath. "I did it. I shot the Wendy-lady," he said quietly, and turned to leave the group.

Just then the boys heard a crowing sound up above. It was Peter's signal. He was back!

They gathered around Wendy so that Peter would not see her. He dropped to the ground in front of them, but no one said a word.

"Why so quiet, boys?" Peter asked.

But still none of the boys spoke.

"Never mind," Peter said. "I have news. I've brought you back a mother! You may even have seen her already. I think she was flying this way."

Tootles cleared his throat. "Boys," he said bravely, "step aside."

The boys obeyed, revealing Wendy's body. Peter bent, took the arrow from Wendy's heart, and turned to face his band of boys.

"Whose arrow is this?" he asked sternly.

"Mine, Peter," Tootles replied.

Angrily, Peter raised the arrow, prepared to hit Tootles with it. But he couldn't do it.

At just that moment, Nibs saw Wendy move. "The Wendy-lady!" he cried. "She moved her arm!"

Peter bent over Wendy again and saw the acorn he had given to her when she'd asked for a kiss. It was on a string around her neck. The arrow had hit the acorn and saved her life!

"Hurry up and get better," he said, "so I can introduce you to the boys and the mermaids."

From her hiding spot up above, Tink sighed loudly.

"Listen to Tink crying because the Wendy-lady is alive," Curly said. The boys told Peter about her crime.

"We are not friends anymore, Tink," Peter cried. "Go away and never come back!"

Frantically, Tinker Bell flew onto Peter's shoulder and begged his forgiveness, but he brushed her off.

Lying on the ground, Wendy stirred slightly. She was waking up.

"I'll be all right," she said wearily. "You don't have to banish her."

"Well, all right," Peter told Tinker Bell. "You can come back, but not for a whole week."

You would think Tinker Bell would be grateful to Wendy for defending her, but Wendy's generosity only made Tink want to pinch her even more. Wendy, in the meantime, was so tired and sore from her hard fall that she rolled onto her side and fell asleep.

"I have an idea," Peter said. "Let's build Wendy a house."

The boys were thrilled; they loved to build. They were incredibly quick carpenters, too, scurrying around for firewood, branches, and twigs, and looking for soft cushiony flowers to use for her bedding.

Just then John and Michael dropped from the sky. They had been sleep-flying, but they woke up as soon as they hit the ground. "Mama?" Michael cried, rubbing his eyes. "Nana?"

"Where are we?" John asked. "Are we dreaming?"

Finally, the boys spotted Peter. "Oh, hello," Peter said distractedly. He had forgotten all about them. Using his feet as a ruler, he bent to measure Wendy to see how big her new house should be.

"Come on," he told her brothers. "We are building a house for Wendy, and you have to help."

"I don't see why Wendy should get her own house," John said. "She's only a girl."

"She's going to be our mother," Curly said. "Now, you heard Peter. Get to work!"

Wendy moved and groaned a bit in her sleep. "Slightly," Peter cried. "Go get a doctor."

Slightly said, "Ay, ay," and left at once, before remembering that there were no doctors on the island. Still, he knew better than to disobey Peter, so he returned wearing John's hat and looking very serious.

Although the other boys knew that Slightly was just pretending, Peter did not. To him, make-believe was the same thing as true. And so, convinced that Slightly was in fact a doctor, he said, "Help this lady. She is very ill."

"I will give her some medicine," said Slightly, bending over the sleeping Wendy and pretending to do just that. "And, there—she is cured!"

"What a relief," Peter said.

While Wendy slept, the boys built her house around her. They knew she would love it because as she slept, she sang: *"I wish I had a pretty house, the smallest ever seen, with bright and shiny reddish walls, and a roof of mossy green."*

As they worked, the boys sang back: *"We've*

built your walls and mossy roof, and made a lovely door. So tell us now, Wendy mother, do you want something more?"

Still sleeping, Wendy sang: *"Well, since you ask, I'd surely grin, for windows all about, with daffodils peeping in, and babies peeping out."*

And so the boys built windows and pulled flowers for Wendy, but they weren't quite sure what to do about the babies.

"Let's just pretend that part," they said.

When they were finished, the house was beautiful, and Wendy was completely contained inside. They were about to go inside to surprise her when they realized they had forgotten to put a knocker on the door.

"Silly donkeys!" Tinker Bell cried from above.

Tootles gave the sole of his shoe to hang on the door, which did the trick. Now there was nothing left to do but knock.

"Everyone stand up straight," Peter warned, "and be on your best behavior."

He knocked politely, and all of the boys waited.

When Wendy opened the door, blinking sleepily, the boys whipped off their hats and bowed.

"Where am I?" she said, confused and surprised.

The boys practically tumbled over one another to explain.

"We built you this house," Slightly said.

"Do you like it?" asked Nibs.

"It's lovely," she said, looking around. "How did you know it's exactly what I wanted?"

"Just clever, I guess," said Slightly. He saw no need to tell her what she had been singing in her sleep.

"Can we be your children?" the twins asked.

"Well," Wendy said, "that's awfully nice of

you, but I am only a child myself. I have no real experience."

"That's okay," Peter said, although he actually knew less about mothers than any of them. "We just need a nice motherly person. You'll do."

Wendy agreed to try, and invited all the boys into her new house. As they gathered around, she did her first motherly thing and told them the end of "Cinderella." When she was finished, she followed the boys to their cave and tucked them in for the evening before returning to her own home.

CHAPTER 8

Something Worse than the Night

࿔

The next morning, the Darling children were measured for their trees. Hook, if you recall, thought it silly to have one tree for each lost boy, but it actually made a great deal of sense. Each different-size boy had a door that fit him as perfectly as a tailored suit. This way, they could all enter the cave at once, without having to wait in line. More important, no other body except each lost boy's exact body could fit in that particular tree. This was especially helpful in case of sneak pirate attacks!

After a few days' practice, the Darling children became very quick and graceful about using their trees. To enter the cave, they sucked their breath in, and down they went at exactly the right speed. To rise, they sucked in and blew out and so wiggled up.

They also grew to love their new underground home. It was simple and sweet, a bit like camping. Even Wendy stayed there now. It was lonely in her own house, and this felt so much more like a real family. The cave was one large, cozy room with a floor made of dirt. The boys used mushrooms as chairs and a sawed-off tree trunk as a table.

There was one big bed, on which all the boys (except Michael) slept, packed in like sardines in a tin. Because space was so tight, there was a strict rule against turning around until one boy gave the signal, and then everyone had to turn at once.

Michael could have slept in the bed, too — there was always room in Neverland for one more — but he was the littlest and Wendy liked to pretend that he was her baby, so she hung him in a basket next to her bed. Her pet wolf, who followed her everywhere, slept on the floor, guarding them both.

Tinker Bell also lived in the cave, in a tiny space carved into the wall, no larger than a bird cage. Over the entrance to her room hung a curtain that she could pull shut when she wanted privacy. Small as it was, Tink's room was the fanciest part of the whole cave, filled with the finest fabrics, soft tiny bedspreads, and delicately carved antique furniture.

"Your house may be bigger," Tinker Bell informed Wendy, "but mine is better."

Still, Wendy had bigger concerns than whether Tink's house was better. The boys kept her so busy, cooking and cleaning and sewing, that weeks would sometimes go by before she left the cave and saw daylight. *It makes one long for the old single life,* she thought wistfully, as a real grown-up might.

As for her parents, she missed them and worried about them, but there was something about Neverland that made time and those worries blur. Somehow, she was confident that the bedroom window—and her parents' arms—would always remain open for her to fly back into.

What did disturb Wendy, however, was the fact that John was starting to forget their parents—and Michael had already forgotten them entirely. He actually thought she was his real mother!

To fix this, Wendy set up a little school, with their old life as the subject instead of spelling or math.

The other boys wanted to go to school, too, so

she let them sit in. Of course, they always failed the quizzes, especially the ones with hard questions like "What color are Mother's eyes?" "How did we spend last Christmas?" and "Describe Father's laugh."

Peter never came to school or took a quiz. He said it was because he despised mothers and holidays and even, sometimes, laughs—but really it was that he couldn't read or write.

While the other boys were in school, Peter would go off alone. Whether he went on real or imaginary adventures, Wendy could never tell unless she or one of the other boys had also gone—and, with Peter, sometimes not even then. But Wendy had many of her own adventures.

Which such tale would you now like to hear? The night attack by the Indians on the underground cave, when a few of them got stuck in the hollow trees like fat Santas in chimneys? Or perhaps the time Peter saved Tiger Lily's life in the mermaid lagoon, and so made her a lifelong friend?

Maybe I should tell you, instead, about the cake the pirates baked and kept leaving around to make the boys sick, but which Wendy kept finding and snatching from the hands of her children until it got stale and they didn't want it anymore and Hook eventually tripped over the hard stale lump in the dark, stubbing his toe.

I could tell you about the birds that were Peter's friends, especially the Never bird who lived in the tree above the lagoon, and how her nest fell in the water once, but she kept sitting on it anyway, to protect her eggs, and Peter gave orders that no one was to disturb her.

A shorter lagoon adventure, and almost as exciting, was Tinker Bell's attempt—with the help of some other fairies—to float a sleeping Wendy back to the mainland on a leaf, until

Wendy woke up and swam back to Neverland, foiling Tink again.

Perhaps the best way to choose is simply to toss a coin. And so the lagoon has won.

If you are lucky, when you close your eyes at night you will sometimes see a lovely lagoon where the mermaids live and sing their beautiful songs. When you are awake, the nearest you can get to this lagoon is the beach, at sunset, in the surf.

The children spent long summer days at the lagoon, swimming or lazily floating. Much to Wendy's disappointment, the mermaids turned out to be as unfriendly as Tinker Bell. When they weren't splashing her with their tails, they ignored her entirely.

The mermaids didn't like the boys, either — except, of course, Peter. Peter spent hours talking to the mermaids or sitting on their tails when they got particularly cheeky.

The lagoon was most beautiful at night, when the moon came up and the mermaids began to sing their strange, wailing songs to lure sailors onto the rocks. But it was not a safe place for humans then.

Wendy knew this, and made sure that she always gathered her children and left before dark. On this day, however, as they were all dozing on Marooners' Rock after lunch, something strange and frightening happened.

It wasn't night yet—at least Wendy didn't think it was—but the lagoon seemed to shift around them. Little shivers ran over the water, and shadows replaced the sun.

It was not night that had come. It was something worse.

CHAPTER 9

The Mermaid Lagoon

ᘡ

Wendy probably should have woken the children at once, but she was a young mother and it had not yet been half an hour since they had eaten. Even when she heard the sound of muffled oars she did not wake them, although she was so scared that her heart seemed to leap into her throat. Instead, she stood guard over them while they digested.

Peter, however—who was snoozing on the rock as well—could smell danger even in his sleep. At the sound of the oars, he jumped to his feet, as alert as a dog, and quickly woke the boys.

"Pirates," he whispered. Just that one, awful word. The others huddled close around him.

"Dive!" he cried. "Now!"

There was a flash of legs, and all of the boys were in the water. They hid as best they could while the pirate dinghy pulled up to the rock they had just been sitting on. In the boat were Smee and Starkey, and their captive, the Indian princess Tiger Lily.

The pirates had caught her trying to sneak

aboard their ship with a knife, and had tied her hands and ankles. They were going to leave Tiger Lily on the rock to drown when the tide came up and covered it.

She did not beg. A true princess, she sat up straight and stared proudly ahead.

In her dark, watery hiding spot, Wendy cried. She had never witnessed such cruelty—or bravery.

Peter had seen plenty of both, and was not particularly moved. What he did hate, however, was unfairness, and this was two against one. It would have been easy for him to wait until the pirates were gone to rescue Tiger Lily, but Peter never chose the easy way out.

"Ahoy there, you rascals," he cried out in his best imitation of Captain Hook's voice.

"Captain?" the two pirates called back, squinting into the darkness.

"He must be swimming out to us," Starkey said.

"We are putting Tiger Lily onto the rock," Smee called.

"Set her free immediately," was the surprising answer, "or I'll plunge my hook into you both."

The command made no sense to the pirates, but they were afraid to disobey their captain. They cut Tiger Lily's cords, and with one last look she slid into the water like a graceful eel.

"Boat ahoy!" Hook yelled suddenly. Only this time it was the real Hook, who was apparently also in the water and swimming toward the boat.

Wendy and Peter watched from the dark water as Hook used his metal claw to grip the side of the boat and pull himself aboard. From the light of the pirates' lantern, Wendy could see his roughly handsome face. She wanted desperately to swim away, but Peter signaled for her to stay put.

Once on board, Hook sat with his head in his hands, groaning in extreme frustration.

"Captain, what's wrong?" Smee asked.

"It's over," Hook said, sighing. "The lost boys have found a mother."

Wendy puffed up with pride, floating now a little higher.

"O evil day!" Starkey said.

"What's a mother?" asked Smee.

Just then, the nest belonging to the Never bird floated by, with the mother bird still sitting on it.

"That is a mother, and a good example of one at that," Hook told Smee. "Her nest fell into the water, but has she deserted her eggs? No."

There was a break in Hook's voice, as if—for one moment—he was recalling his childhood and his own mother. But he brushed away this weakness and what might have been a small tear with his hook.

"Captain, I propose we kidnap the boys' mother and make her our own," Smee suggested.

"Yes," Hook said. "We will capture the boys and make them walk the plank! Then we will keep their mother."

Smee and Starkey cheered.

"Wait," Hook said suddenly, remembering Tiger Lily. "Where's the princess?"

"We let her go," Smee replied.

"Why?" Hook demanded.

"Why, you told us to," Smee stammered.

"I heard you, too, Captain," Starkey said.

"What kind of trickery is going on here?" thundered Hook. "I gave no such order." He looked around and shivered. "Dark spirit that haunts the lagoon tonight," he called out. "Do you hear me?"

"I hear you," Peter replied in Hook's own voice.

Hook was brave, but Smee and Starkey hugged each other, shaking.

"Who are you?" Hook called out.

"I am James Hook," replied the voice, "captain of the *Jolly Roger.*"

"No, you aren't!" Hook screamed angrily.

"Yes, I am," the voice insisted.

"If you are Hook," Hook said, trying to sound friendly, "then who am I?"

"You are a codfish," Peter said promptly.

Smee and Starkey were slightly stupid, and proud—a bad combination. "A codfish?" they muttered. "Have we been taking orders all this time from a mere fish?"

Hook barely heard them. It was not their lack of faith in him that most bothered him but, suddenly, his lack of faith in himself. He felt his ego slipping away from him. "Don't desert me," he whispered to it, hoarsely.

"Hook," Hook asked cleverly, "do you have another voice?"

Peter could never resist a game, so he answered in his own voice, "I do."

"And another name?"

"Yes."

"Are you an animal, vegetable, or mineral?" Hook asked.

"Yes, no, and no," Peter replied.

"Are you a man?" Hook tried next.

"No," Peter practically spit.

"A boy, then?"

"Yes."

"An ordinary boy?"

Wendy wanted to play, too. "He is a wonderful boy!" she shouted out, giggling.

Hook was stumped.

"You can't guess, you can't guess," Peter bragged. "Give up?"

In Peter's pride, the pirates saw their chance.

"Yes, we give up," they cried. "Tell us who you are."

"I'm Peter Pan!" Peter yelled out, laughing.

Instantly Hook was himself once more, and Smee and Starkey his faithful crew.

"Get him!" Hook roared. "Dead or alive!"

Quickly Peter whistled for his own crew. The lost boys were resting in various parts of the lagoon.

"We're coming, Peter," they cried.

The fight was short but sharp. Swords flew in the water and air, followed by many wheezes and whoops and wails as the two pirates and the lost boys clashed.

Hook and Peter had their own private battle to fight. They met not in the water but on the rock—which they both, coincidentally, climbed at the same time, from opposite sides. It was so dark that they didn't see each other until they were almost in the middle, nose-to-nose.

Peter grabbed a knife from Hook's belt and was about to finish him off when he noticed that he was higher up on the rock than Hook. This would not have been fighting fair, so Peter offered Hook a hand to hoist himself up.

Hook was not a similar fan of fighting fair. He leaned over and bit Peter in response.

It was not the pain of the bite but the pain and surprise of the unfairness that dazed Peter, making him quite helpless. All children are affected like this the first time they realize the world is unfair. People had been unfair to Peter before, but he had always forgotten it, and so he reacted as if it were the first time.

Hook clawed Peter twice with his hook, and might have finished him off had he not just then heard a ticking. Instead, Hook slid immediately into the water, swimming madly for his ship.

CHAPTER 10

The Never Bird

∽

Out on the water, the lost boys had won their fight with Smee and Starkey, but they couldn't find Peter or Wendy or Hook. Taking the pirates' dinghy, they sailed home in it, shouting for Peter and Wendy the entire time. But there was no response, except for an occasional mocking from the mermaids.

"They must be swimming or flying back," the boys concluded.

Had they stayed in the lagoon, they might have soon heard two voices crying for help. Peter and Wendy—he injured and she weak—had climbed back onto Marooners' Rock. As the water rose dangerously around them, they fell unconscious one right after the other.

A mischievous mermaid pulled Wendy by her toe, trying to get her into the water. Feeling her slip from him, Peter woke up just in time to pull her back.

"Our rock is shrinking," he told her. "Soon it will be gone."

"Let's go, then!" Wendy cried. "We can swim or fly away."

"I can do neither," Peter replied. "I have been injured. You go."

But Wendy was too weak to make it on her own. The children put their hands over their eyes to shut out the sight of the rising water, and prepared to meet their end.

Just then something brushed Peter's leg. It

was as light as a feather, and it seemed to be asking, *Can I help?*

What luck! It was the tail of a kite, which Michael had made a few days earlier but then lost to the wind. Peter grabbed it and wrapped it around Wendy.

"Now you!" Wendy cried.

"It can't lift us both," Peter explained. "Michael and Curly tried."

Wendy clung to Peter, refusing to go without him, but he pushed her from the rock and away she flew. Peter was left all alone in the lagoon.

The rock grew smaller and smaller. In the distance, the mermaids called sadly to the moon. Like any boy, Peter was scared to die. But soon his fear changed to excitement. "To die will be an awfully big adventure," he said.

Around him, the lagoon grew quieter and quieter. Peter heard the mermaids saying good night to one another and shutting the doors to their coral caves. He heard the water gurgle greedily as it rose to nibble on the rock. Then he saw something white floating on the water. He thought it was a piece of paper, or perhaps a piece of Michael's kite. But as he continued to stare at it, he realized that it had a more definite sense of purpose than a mere piece of paper would have. It seemed to be fighting the tide instead of just going with the flow. Peter found himself rooting for the white streak to win.

The piece of paper was actually the Never bird, still sitting on her now-floating nest. She was trying desperately to reach Peter. Although he had teased her in the past, he had also given orders that her nest was not to be disturbed. For this reason, and perhaps because she was above all things a mother, she would disturb her nest herself—to save his life.

"Swim to the nest," she called to him. "I am too tired to row all the way to you."

But Peter didn't speak bird language, and couldn't understand her. And, even near death, he could be very impatient.

"What are you quacking about?" Peter asked rudely. "I don't understand a word!"

"Why, I never!" the Never bird said, and tried again.

"Same to you!" Peter replied. "Whatever you just said!"

Remembering that he was only a child, the maternal Never bird took a deep breath and made one last push to row her nest to the rock. Upon reaching it, she flew up, leaving her eggs behind to make some room for Peter.

Finally realizing her meaning, Peter waved his thank-you to the Never bird. Looking down, however, he saw there was not enough room in the nest for both him and her two large white eggs.

He lifted the eggs up, and the Never bird covered her eyes with her feathers, afraid of what Peter might do.

On the rock next to Peter was a waterproof hat, broad and wide, which Starkey had left behind. Peter put the eggs into the hat and set them afloat. With a final happy quack, the Never bird swooped down and settled herself on top of her eggs.

Peter got into the Never bird's old nest, waved good-bye, and pushed off. He in his nest and Wendy with her kite arrived back at the cave at nearly the same time.

Oh, how everyone rejoiced! The party went on until Wendy realized how late it was and told everyone it was well past their bedtime.

The boys tried to stall, insisting they were injured and in need of slings and bandages, but Wendy would have none of it and sent them to bed.

CHAPTER 11

The Happy Family

On the night that would come to be known as "the night of all nights," the children ate a make-believe dinner. Unfortunately, their hunger was real, and as a result they were noisy and misbehaving.

"Be quiet!" Wendy yelled finally, for she was hungry and grumpy, too. "Is your plate empty, Slightly?"

Slightly looked down at his imaginary plate. "Not quite, Mommy."

"He didn't take one bite of his carrots," Nibs said.

John raised his hand. "Since Peter isn't here, can I sit in his chair?"

"Sit in Father's chair? No," replied Wendy, who had taken to referring to Peter as Father.

"He's not our real father," John complained.

Tootles wanted in, too. "Can I be the father?" he asked.

"No," Wendy said.

"What about the baby?" he asked.

"I'm the baby," Michael said. He was already settled in his comfortable basket.

Tootles moped.

"Slightly has his elbows on the table," some-one reported.

"The twins ate their dessert before their vegetables," someone else added.

"Curly is eating all the butter and honey."

"Nibs is speaking with his mouth full."

Wasn't this just like normal family life? Later, after the imaginary dishes were washed, Wendy sat by the fire and sewed socks with very real holes in them. As her boys played around her, she felt very content with her familiar little family. Just one thing was missing.

Suddenly she heard a step above them.

"That's Peter's step," Wendy said. "Children, go greet Father at the door."

Peter entered, dropping down through his own personal tree, and the children ran to him happily. He had brought nuts and treats for them and—from the crocodile—the correct time for Wendy. This he obtained by following the crocodile until he chimed the hour.

"You spoil us, Peter," Wendy said.

"We want to dance!" the twins cried.

"Go ahead," said Peter, who was in a jolly mood.

"You and Mommy, too!"

"Come on, Peter," Wendy said. "Children, go put your nightgowns on first."

While the boys ran to do so, Peter and Wendy had a quiet moment alone.

"Life is good, isn't it?" Peter said, warming his feet by the fire. "You and me, and the little ones?"

"It is," Wendy agreed. "I think Curly has your nose."

"Michael takes after you," Peter said.

But suddenly, Peter looked scared.

"Wendy," he said. "This is all make-believe, right? I'm not really their father?"

Wendy looked at him for a few seconds.

"It's make-believe," she finally said.

"Whew!" Peter cried. "I can't tell you how relieved I am to hear that! It would make me feel so old to be their real father!"

"And how do you feel about me?" Wendy asked.

Peter just blinked, as if he didn't quite understand the question.

Wendy sighed and went to sit at the other end of the room, with her back to him. At that moment, the boys came out and sang and danced for Peter and Wendy in their nightgowns. When they had finished dancing, the boys got into bed for Wendy's good-night story—the story that they loved best, and which Peter hated. Usually when she told this story, he put his hands over his ears or left the room. Tonight, however, he stayed to listen.

"Once upon a time there was a gentleman," Wendy began.

"I want a lady," Curly said.

"I want a white rat," said Nibs.

"Shhh," Wendy said. "Okay, there was a lady as well. Their names were Mr. and Mrs. Darling."

On the other side of the room, Peter flinched.

"Hey," John said, "I know them."

"Me too," Michael said, but he didn't sound sure.

"Mr. and Mrs. Darling were married and had three—"

"White rats?" Nibs cried hopefully.

"Children," Wendy said. "And they had a nurse called Nana. But one day Mr. Darling got mad at Nana and chained her up in the yard, and so all the children flew away to Neverland."

"That is a great story," said Nibs.

"Imagine how sad these parents were after their children left," Wendy said.

"Poor parents," the boys moaned, but they were just pretending to feel sorry.

"It's an awfully sad story," the first twin said cheerfully.

"If you knew how strong a mother's love is, you wouldn't worry," Wendy said.

And now she came to the part that Peter hated the most.

"You see," Wendy said, "the mother left the window open so her children could fly back one day." She closed her eyes. "Can't you see it? Can't you picture the happy scene when the children finally fly back home?"

From Peter's corner came a hollow groan.

"Are you in pain?" Wendy asked.

"No, but you are wrong about mothers." He took a deep breath. "A long time ago, I thought my mother would also keep the window open for me, so I stayed away and played. But when I flew back, the window was locked. She had forgotten all about me, and another little boy was sleeping in my bed."

"Is that true or make-believe?" Wendy asked, alarmed.

Peter wasn't sure, but it scared the children all the same. *So that is what mothers are like,* they thought.

"Wendy, let's go home right now!" John cried. "Maybe it's too late and the window's already locked!"

"Yes," she said, clutching her brothers. She

was so worried about the closed window that she didn't even think about Peter's feelings. "Peter, will you arrange it?"

"If you like," he replied coolly, as if she had asked him to pass the nuts. After all, if she didn't care, neither would he!

Upset at the idea of losing their mother, the lost boys surrounded Wendy threateningly.

"We won't let you go!" they cried. "We'll keep you prisoner!"

"Tootles, help!" Wendy cried. Somehow, even though he was the silliest boy, she knew he was the right person to ask.

Tootles stepped between her and the rest of the boys. "You'll have to go through me first," he said.

Peter spoke up. "We keep no girls here against their will. Since flying makes you so tired, I'll have the Indians guide you through the woods. Then Tink can take you across the sea."

"Thank you, Peter," Wendy said. She turned to the lost boys. "Come with us," she offered. "I am sure my parents would adopt you."

This was meant mainly for Peter, but all of the boys jumped with joy.

"Peter, can we go?" they pleaded.

"If you like," he repeated bitterly, and they rushed to pack. He, however, didn't move.

"Go pack, Peter," Wendy said, her voice low.

"I'm not going," he replied. Then, to show that he didn't care, he skipped around the room singing.

"But we can find your mother," Wendy begged.

"No! I don't like mothers! She would only tell me I have to grow up and stop having fun."

The other boys watched this exchange nervously. Peter not coming? What would they do? Could they still go? Did they want to?

"Now, then," Peter said, "I'll have no fuss, no blubbering good-byes. It was a pleasure to meet you, Wendy." He held out his hand formally.

"You'll take good care of yourself?" she asked.

"Yes. Ready, Tinker Bell?"

Tinker Bell groaned from her cave. She resented having to help Wendy, but at least the girl would finally be gone.

"Then off you go."

At just that moment, however, there was a clashing sound above. The pirates had attacked the Indians. The trip home was off, at least for now.

CHAPTER 12

Extremely Happy Hook

The pirate attack was a complete surprise. Hook had broken all of the rules the pirates and the Indians normally followed when they fought. He attacked in neither the time nor the place that was allowed. When it was over, almost all of the Indians were injured. Only Tiger Lily managed to escape unharmed.

Finished with the Indians, the pirates still could not rest. It was, after all, not the Indians they had come for. The Indians were just bees to be smoked out so they could get to the honey.

The pirates wanted the lost boys and Wendy and, most of all, Peter Pan.

Peter was an awfully small boy to inspire such a big hatred in Hook, even if he *had* thrown Hook's hand to the crocodile. But there was something about him that enraged Hook. It was more than Peter's courage, or his cuteness. It was his cockiness, his absolute confidence in himself. This is something many children have, but most grownups have lost it entirely. Perhaps Hook had lost some of his, too, and wanted it back.

The question was: How could the pirates get down the hollow trees, which were perfectly sized to allow each individual lost boy down but no one else?

Below, the boys were still trying to figure out who had won the battle. "If it was the Indians," they reasoned, "they will beat their tom-tom drums. It is always their sign of victory."

Perched at the edge of the hollow trees up

PETER PAN

above, the pirates heard this. Smee happened to be sitting on a tom-tom, which Hook ordered him to beat immediately. After a moment of confusion, Smee understood and smiled.

BANG! BANG! BANG! went the tom-tom drum.

"The tom-tom!" the pirates heard Peter cry. "The Indians have won! Let's go up and celebrate with them!"

The lost boys cheered, and Hook ordered his men to take their positions and get ready for the boys to come up through their trees.

The first to emerge was Curly. The pirates threw him around like a ball—from Cecco to Smee, then Starkey, then Bill Jukes, then Noodler.

One by one, all of the boys were plucked from their trees and tossed around in this manner. It was, to say the least, a different kind of flying than they were used to. The pirates then gagged the boys and tied them up.

With Wendy, the pirates behaved differently. After all, she was a lady—or, rather, a little girl—and even pirates have some manners. When she emerged, Hook offered her his arm and bowed so elegantly that she blushed. When they tied her up, they used the softest rope they had, apologizing and making sure that they weren't hurting her.

When it came time to tie up Slightly, however, the pirates found that it took far more rope than it had for the other boys or Wendy. It turned out that Slightly had been sneaking so many snacks lately that he had grown greatly. In fact, there had come a day when he no longer fit in his tree.

How had he gotten into and out of the cave? Each night while the other boys slept, he had secretly started to widen the hole in his tree.

"Why are you so much bigger than the other boys?" Hook demanded. "Why, you're practically as big as a grown-up."

While the pirates found extra rope with which to tie him up, Hook had a brilliant idea. He knew how he was going to get Peter, who was still down in the cave.

He signaled for the other pirates to take the lost boys and Wendy to the ship and leave him alone to his plans. Tiptoeing over to Slightly's tree, Hook saw that it was now wide enough to let him through. He listened for any sound from down below, but all was quiet. Was Peter asleep? Was he waiting at the bottom of the tree with his dagger in his hand?

The only way to find out was to try. Hook took a deep breath, stepped into the tree, and let himself fall. When he hit the ground, he crouched for a second, waiting for his eyes to adjust to the dark of the underground cave. Finally, things began to take shape. In the corner, he saw the great bed and, on it, Peter sleeping.

For once, Peter wasn't pretending. He was unaware of what was happening up above. He believed the Indians had won the battle, and that the lost boys had gone up to celebrate with them.

He was happy for the Indians, but the lost boys were going to leave him, and Peter didn't feel like celebrating. Oh, he had pretended not to care, but he was very sad. And when he got sad, he got sleepy. Today he was so sleepy that he didn't even dream.

It was in this sad, deep, dreamless sleep that Hook found Peter. As he stood over the bed and looked down, Hook felt slightly sorry for the boy. After all, Peter was only a child, and Hook wasn't completely evil.

But then Peter smiled in his sleep—perhaps he was dreaming something after all—and that smile seemed so arrogant, it made Hook angry all over again.

Hook saw a glass of water on Peter's night table and knew exactly what to do. In case he should ever be captured, Hook always carried a small bottle of poison with him. Taking it out of his pocket now, he added a few drops to Peter's water. Peter would wake up, take a sip, and fall to the ground dead.

With one last satisfied look back, Hook climbed back up Slightly's tree. Once above ground, Hook tilted his captain's hat at a fashionable angle, wound his dark cloak dramatically around himself, and stole away through the forest.

CHAPTER 13

Carried Off

Peter slept for a long time. Finally, he was awakened by a soft rapping on the door of his tree. When he opened his eyes, it was still dark. He felt for his sword.

"Who is it?" he asked.

There was no answer, only another knock.

"I said, who is it?"

Still nothing, only silence.

Peter was scared, but also excited. He loved adventures, especially ones that placed him in danger. His heart beat very fast. "I won't open unless you speak," he said.

"Let me in, Peter," the visitor finally said in a lovely bell-like voice.

It was Tinker Bell! Peter quickly unlocked the door and she flew in, her face flushed and her pretty dress stained with mud.

Tinker Bell told Peter that Wendy and the boys had been captured and were now prisoners on the pirate ship.

"I must save her!" Peter cried, leaping for his weapons.

But first he would have a sip of the water Wendy had left by his bed. His hand reached for the glass.

"No!" Tinker Bell cried, for she had heard Hook mutter about his trick as he sped through the forest. "It is poisoned!"

"What? How? By whom?"

"Hook."

"Don't be silly. How could Hook have gotten down here?"

"I don't know, but he did."

Peter Pan was stubborn, and thirsty, so he raised his glass anyway. Tinker Bell flew quickly between his lips and the glass and took a sip of the water instead.

"Hey, that's my water," Peter protested.

Tinker Bell did not answer. She was already spinning dizzily in the air, poisoned.

"Tink?" Peter asked, suddenly afraid.

"You should have listened to me," Tinker Bell said weakly.

"Oh, Tink, why did you risk your life to save me?" Peter asked.

Her wings were weak, but she managed to land gracefully on Peter's shoulder and give his nose one last loving pinch. She whispered in his

ear, "Because I love you, you silly donkey." Then she flew weakly back to her little cave and collapsed on her bed.

Peter knelt near Tinker Bell's limp body in distress. His head filled almost the entire space of her room. Tink's light was growing darker. Peter knew she would die if it went out entirely.

"Oh, Tink," he cried, "what can I do? I need you. Please don't leave me now."

"I think I could get well again if children believed in fairies," Tinker Bell gasped.

But there were no children left in the cave! Peter stood up straight and screamed out to all of the children in the universe, to all who might be dreaming about Neverland, boys and girls in their pajamas, safe in their beds—maybe even you.

"Do you believe?" he cried, and his question rang throughout the world. Tink sat up weakly in bed and listened, straining to hear her fate. She and Peter thought they heard some voices, but they weren't sure.

"If you believe," Peter tried next, "clap your hands. Don't let Tink die!"

This time they heard their answer: many children clapping. A few naughty, nasty children hissed, but mostly they clapped—until, that is, the clapping suddenly stopped, having been hushed by worried mothers who had rushed into bedrooms to find out what all the commotion was about.

Nevertheless, that bit of clapping was enough. Tinker Bell was saved. Back to her old self, she didn't even think of thanking the children who believed—although she did want revenge on the few who had hissed.

"Now we must rescue Wendy!" Peter vowed. Oh, if only some clapping could work that magic as well.

"Yes, yes, we must always think of Wendy," Tinker Bell said glumly.

It was a cloudy night, not good weather for flying, so Peter pressed forward on the ground, in Indian fashion. He could not help but notice that the island was strangely quiet, as though it were still in shock from the recent battle.

As Peter walked, he looked for things the boys might have dropped. He had trained them, if ever taken, to leave such clues. Slightly, for example, was to cut trees and Curly to drop seeds. Wendy knew to drop her handkerchief.

But he saw nothing.

He swore a terrible oath: "Hook or me this time!"

CHAPTER 14

The Pirate Ship

᠃

The *Jolly Roger* lurked low in the water like a waiting crocodile. The pirates sat on deck in the cool fog of the night, playing cards or napping. Hook could not play, or rest. Distracted, he paced the deck. It wasn't that he was unhappy. After all, Peter had been removed, and the lost boys were soon to walk the plank. And yet, for some reason, his happiness was incomplete.

Like Mr. Darling, Hook worried about things like breeding and class—what he liked to call "good form." He, too, cared very much what people—especially people with good form—thought about him.

Whenever he did something, or wanted something, he would ask himself, *Is it good form to do or want such a thing?* Sometimes he worried that it was not good form to think so much about good form.

But Hook wasn't just unhappy; he was also lonely. As hard as it was to believe, Hook hurt. He had no children to love him. It was strange that this should bother him, but it was true all the same.

In a way, Hook envied Smee. Smee was the least threatening of the pirates, and yet the children loved him. Michael had even tried on his spectacles. Thinking about the children's preference for Smee made Hook angry, and he decided to finish off the boys once and for all.

"Are the children tied up so they can't fly away?" he yelled.

"Ay, ay," came the reply.

"Well, then, hoist them up!"

The boys were brought up on deck before him.

"Six of you will walk the plank tonight," Hook announced, "but I have room for two cabin boys. Who will it be? Which of you will come to work for me?"

Tootles stepped forward. "I would, sir, but I don't think my mother would want me to be a pirate. Would yours, Slightly?"

"I don't think so," Slightly said.

The twins agreed, as did the others. None of their mothers would approve.

"Enough!" Hook cried. He pointed to John. "You!" he said. "You look like you have a little pluck in you. Do you want to be a pirate?"

Secretly, John had always dreamed of being a pirate. He even had a pirate name picked out: Red-Handed Jack. In a low voice, he now confessed this to Hook.

"Why, Red-Handed Jack is a fine name!" Hook said.

"What would my name be if I joined?" Michael asked.

"Blackbeard Joe," Hook said.

Michael was impressed.

"Will we still be respectful subjects of the king of England?" John asked.

"No!" Hook replied. "You would have to swear, *Down with the king!*"

"Oh," John said, his face falling. He could never turn his back on England. "Well, then, never mind."

"Then you shall walk the plank, too!" Hook roared.

The boys went pale as they saw Jukes and Cecco preparing the piece of wood off which they would walk before falling into the water. But they tried to look brave, especially when Wendy was brought up.

She was the brave one. She emerged from belowdecks wearing a dark scowl.

"Are you ready to watch your boys walk the plank?" Hook asked her sweetly. "Do you have any last words for them?"

"I do," Wendy replied in a loud, clear voice. "I have a message from their real mothers, and it is a hope that their sons will die bravely and with their heads held high, like proper English gentlemen."

The boys all stood up a little higher, trying to be brave, to do this one last thing for their mothers and Wendy.

"Tie her up to the mast," Hook yelled, and Smee obeyed.

"I'll save you if you promise to be my mother," Smee whispered to Wendy.

"I would rather have no children at all," she replied scornfully, even though she had to admit that Smee was the nicest pirate of them all.

The boys tried to be brave as they were put on the plank. In the end, however, they were only little boys, and they could not stop themselves from shaking and shivering with fear.

Wendy turned her head. She couldn't look.

Hook took a step toward her. He wanted her to watch the boys walk, one by one, off the end of the plank. But he never reached her. He never got to hear her beg for the boys' lives. Instead he heard *tick, tick, tick.* It was the terrible tick, he realized, of the crocodile.

All eyes were suddenly on Hook. It was almost a sad sight to see this brave pirate captain positively freeze in terror as the ticking sound came nearer and nearer. Even his claw hung inactive, as if it, too, were afraid.

Hook fell to the deck and crawled as far from the sound as he could go.

"Hide me," he begged, and the pirates gathered grimly around him in the center of the boat.

The lost boys glanced over the side of the boat to look for the crocodile, but to their surprise they saw Peter approaching instead!

He signaled them not to give any sign, and kept on ticking and climbing.

CHAPTER 15

Hook or Me This Time!

Odd things often happen without us even noticing. Such was the case with Peter's ticking. A few minutes earlier, on his way to the boat, Peter had passed by the crocodile and noticed that he was no longer making noise. After a moment's thought, he realized that the clock must have finally wound down.

Peter knew that the beasts on the island feared the crocodile and avoided the ticking sound. Without even thinking about it, he began to imitate the ticking so that he could pass through the forest unbothered. The crocodile heard this, and perhaps because he missed the sound, he began to follow Peter.

As Peter swam, newly ticking, to the boat, he had one thought about the upcoming battle: *Hook or me this time.* Only one of them would walk away alive, he vowed.

One of the pirates spotted Peter as he was climbing up the side of the boat. Before he could cry out, John clamped his hands over the pirate's mouth. The other boys quickly caught him and tossed him overboard with a gentle splash.

The pirates were now looking over the other side of the boat, searching for the crocodile. Peter, who had temporarily stopped ticking, tiptoed into a cabin belowdecks.

"I think it's gone, Captain," Smee said.

"Well, then, here's to Johnny Plank!" Hook cried, in an even worse mood now because the boys had seen him scared.

He started to sing: *"Yo ho, yo ho, the frisky plank, you walks along it so, till it goes down and you goes down to the dark water below!"*

Hook paused.

"Now, tell me," he said, not unkindly. "Would you like a bit of a snack before you go? There are some sandwiches in the cabin."

"No!" the boys cried, not only because they weren't hungry, but because Peter was hiding in the cabin.

"I can't very well send you off to the depths below on empty stomachs, can I?" Hook asked. "Jukes, go get the sandwiches."

"Ay, ay," Jukes said, and went inside.

Within seconds there was a dreadful cry from inside the cabin. The cry was followed by a strange crowing sound, which confused the pirates but which the boys understood perfectly.

"What is that noise?" Hook asked. "Is that a bird? Someone go check on Bill Jukes."

The Italian Cecco went inside for a peek and then ran out, pale. "Bill Jukes is gone," he reported.

"Gone?" the other pirates asked.

"I can't see what—it's too dark in there—but there's something in there, crowing," Cecco said.

"Go and bring it to me," Hook demanded.

"Don't make me," Cecco cried, but seeing Hook flex his claw, Cecco obeyed.

Within seconds there was another screech and then more crowing.

"Who's going to bring me that rooster?" Hook demanded. "Did you volunteer, Starkey? My hook seems to think you did."

"I'd rather swing," Starkey said in a low voice, and the rest of the pirates mumbled their agreement.

"Is this mutiny?" Hook said. "With Starkey as the ringleader?" He extended his claw. "Perhaps you would like to shake my hand, Starkey," he said.

Starkey looked around for help but found none. Hook advanced with a gleam in his eye. Before Hook could get him, Starkey jumped on the pirates' cannon, shimmied out to its edge, and threw himself into the sea.

"Never mind," Hook muttered. "I'll go get that rooster myself!"

A minute later, Hook came staggering out without his lantern.

"Something blew out my light," he said, shaking. "And Cecco is missing."

Pirates are a superstitious bunch, and this was too much for them.

"This ship's cursed," one of them muttered.

"Haunted," the others agreed.

Knowing it was Peter, Michael giggled. Hook noticed this. It gave him an idea.

"Open the cabin door and push the lost boys in," he suggested. "If they kill the bird, so much the better, and if it kills them, we're none the worse. We're going to kill them anyway."

The boys pretended to cry and struggle as they were pushed inside.

"Now let's listen," Hook said, and the pirates all crowded around the door.

Meanwhile, Peter had found the key to unlock the boys' chains. They looked for weapons while Peter snuck out through an opposite porthole and cut Wendy's bonds.

They could have flown away, but Peter had vowed that it was Hook or him this time. He told Wendy to go hide with the boys, wrapped himself in her cloak, and took her place on the mast.

Then he took a deep breath and crowed.

The pirates were terrified. Had the crow killed all the boys? Would it kill them next?

"Lads," Hook suggested, "perhaps our run of bad luck is due to the lady we have on board. Let's get rid of her and see if our luck changes."

"Throw her overboard," the pirates cried, and rushed at the figure in the cloak.

"There's no one who can save you now," the pirates hissed.

"There's one person," the figure at the mast replied in a strangely low voice. "Peter Pan!"

As he spoke, Peter threw off the cloak and revealed his face. Suddenly everyone understood what was happening.

"Get him!" Hook cried, but not very convincingly. He sensed that Peter was about to best him once again, and it was too much for him. Hook's fierce heart broke.

"Fight!" Peter cried.

The boys burst out of the cabin, and a fierce battle with the pirates began. The pirates were stronger, but the boys were smarter and fought in pairs. Some of the pirates jumped overboard, while others ran away and hid. Finally only Hook was left.

The boys surrounded him.

Even alone, he was strong and brave and kept them away using nothing but his hook. He lifted one boy up with it and used him as a shield.

Peter jumped into the circle.

"Stand back!" he cried. "This man is mine!"

For a long time, the enemies just looked at each other.

"So," Hook said. "This is all your doing."

"It is," Peter crowed.

"Cocky, arrogant boy," Hook said. "Prepare to meet your end."

"And you!" Peter cried.

A dramatic sword fight followed, during which both man and boy fought bravely. Finally,

Hook moved to get Peter with his iron hand. Peter ducked and lunged with his sword, piercing Hook in the ribs.

Hook stared down at the wound in surprise. As you may recall, the only blood he could not stand to look at was his own. He dropped his sword.

"Now," the boys cried. It was time to finish Hook off! They lunged forward, but Peter put up his hand, stopping them.

"Pick up your sword," he told Hook, who obeyed.

"What are you?" Hook asked. "How is it possible that you have beaten me? You cannot be just an ordinary boy."

"I am not an ordinary boy," Peter said. "I am youth. I am joy. I am a little bird that just escaped its shell. And, above all, I am fair."

Hook narrowed his eyes. "Enough," he said. "Back to the fight!"

He swung his sword around wildly. Anyone else would have been hit, but Peter ducked as if the wind were working to protect him, blowing him just the right distance this way and that.

Desperate, Hook ran off and returned with a grenade.

"In two minutes," he cried when he returned, "this ship will be blown to bits!"

But Peter just picked up the grenade and threw it overboard.

Hook hated how calmly and bravely Peter was behaving. Peter was showing . . . could it possibly be . . . good form?

The thought of this was too much to bear. As the boys drew closer, Hook barely even saw them. His mind was elsewhere—back in his school days when he had first learned of good form.

Seeing Peter advancing with his sword, Hook turned and stood at the edge of the boat, looking down at the sea.

He saw that the crocodile was there waiting for him.

Peter kicked him overboard. As Hook fell, he realized, much to his delight, that this kick was actually very bad form. Feeling superior, Hook went happily to the crocodile.

With the fight at last over, Wendy emerged from the cabin below. The boys danced around her, pointing out all of the places where they had fought.

"Yes, yes, you are very brave boys," Wendy said, "but it's past your bedtime. Let's get into the pirates' bunks, messy as they are, and get some rest."

All of the boys went down to sleep except Peter. He fell asleep up on deck, next to the pirates' cannon. Wendy sat next to him the whole time, softly rubbing his head to protect him from bad dreams.

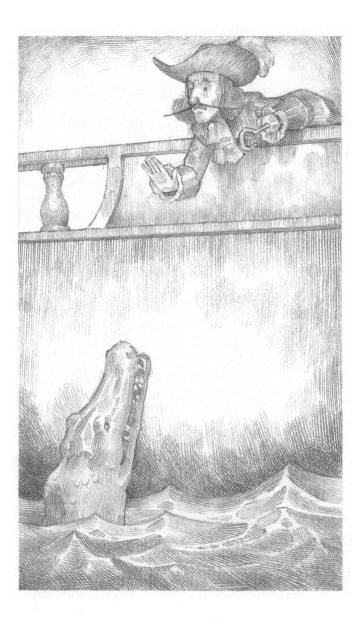

CHAPTER 16

The Return Home

Everyone woke up early next day. It was a very long journey back home and the sea was quite rough, so the going would be slow.

With slight alterations from Wendy, the pirates' clothes fit the boys just fine—pants cut off at the knees and jaunty hats and eye patches. The scowls they added themselves.

Peter, of course, was the captain. Nibs and John were first and second mates. None of the boys had any training in sailing a pirate ship, but they pretended they did—which in Neverland is always enough. As they worked, securing jibs and sheets and all sorts of other sailor words, they sang and cheered heartily. Finally, they got the ship out into the open sea, let loose her sails, and started for England. It was time.

Peter had decided that they would sail as far as the Azore Islands, and then fly the rest of the way. He stood at the wheel and addressed his pirate crew.

"You scum," he cried. "You mangy dogs! There will be no mutiny on my ship, or else!"

The boys knew that Peter was only pretending to be a pirate, but — unlike them — he couldn't always tell the difference. He was even wearing Hook's old clothes. And so they laughed, but nervously.

Let us leave the boys on the boat and travel back to the Darlings' home. It seems a shame to have neglected it all this time. But Mrs. Darling wouldn't have wanted us to focus on her when we could, instead, be keeping an eye on her little ones.

It would serve those naughty children right if their beds were not made and their room was all dusty and their parents weren't even home, having forgotten all about them.

Of course, this is not the case, and this is the kind of thing children count on so they can have their adventures.

The only difference from when they left is that Nana is no longer chained. Mr. Darling could admit when he was wrong. The second the children had flown, he had invited Nana back into the house, where she had stayed.

Then, however, he had done a most unusual thing. He had gone down on all fours and crawled into Nana's kennel himself! Mrs. Darling had begged him to come out, but he had said, "Not until the children come back."

Every morning, the kennel was carried with Mr. Darling in it to the office, and then back again at night. *This is my punishment, and it is proper,* he thought.

Given how much he cared what other people thought of him, it was a hard punishment indeed. People laughed and pointed, peering inside, and he became known as "Darling in the Kennel."

The true beauty of his sacrifice, however, soon shone through. When the public learned why he had confined himself to Nana's kennel, they began to follow him, not to laugh, but to praise. Girls asked for his autograph. Society types invited him to dinner—in his kennel and black tie, of course. KENNEL—one headline in the papers read—THE NEW GOOD FORM. It was what he had always wanted, and yet Mr. Darling could not enjoy his new status in the community.

Mrs. Darling was sad as well. When she managed to fall asleep, usually in her chair by the fire, she would dream of her children. This night was no different.

Tonight, however, let us whisper in her ear that the children are on their way home. But perhaps we should not, because she has wakened with a start, calling out their names.

There is a chill in the air, but the Darlings would never dare close the window. It must always stay open for the children.

Little do they know that, at this moment, there is someone at that window. It is Peter. He has flown ahead, with Tinker Bell.

⌒

"Open," Peter muttered bitterly, upon seeing the window. "I knew it would be."

Peter came up with one final plan. He would fly in quietly—so as not to wake Mr. Darling in his kennel—lock the window, and then sneak out through the front door. That way, when Wendy and the boys arrived, they would think their parents had forgotten about them, and they would have to come back to Neverland.

Oh, this is a brilliant idea! he thought. He didn't care about Wendy's or her mother's feelings—only about what he wanted. Children can be selfish that way.

On his way back out of the house, however, Peter passed Mrs. Darling, sleeping by the fire. Seeing the dried tears on her puffy face, he felt guilty for the first time.

I need her, too! he wanted to shout. *We can't both have her.*

He jumped and sang, and made funny faces, but as hard as he tried, he couldn't get poor Mrs.

133

Darling's tears out of his head. Maybe he was growing up a bit after all. The thought enraged him.

"Oh, fine," he huffed. "C'mon, Tink!" They unbarred the window and flew away.

Moments later, the children found the house and the open window. They landed softly on their old bedroom floor. Michael didn't even recognize the place.

"This looks familiar," he said.

"Of course, silly, it's our room," said John.

"There's Nana's kennel!" Wendy cried, and they all rushed to look inside. But in place of Nana they saw a man.

"It's Father," Wendy said.

"Let me see a father," Michael begged. He didn't remember his father. "Hmmpf," he said, a little disappointed. "The pirates were bigger." It is a good thing Mr. Darling was asleep and didn't hear his son, for it would have broken his heart.

"Did he always sleep in the kennel?" John asked, confused.

Suddenly Wendy couldn't remember, either.

Just then they heard the piano downstairs.

"Mother!" Wendy gasped.

"Aren't you our mother?" Michael asked.

"Oh, dear," Wendy said. Perhaps they had waited too long to come back.

"Let's go downstairs and surprise her," John suggested. "We can yell *boo.*"

"Let's be a bit gentler," Wendy said. "We owe her that much. Let's get into our beds and she'll come in and find us."

And that is exactly what they did.

CHAPTER 17

Growing Up and Good-Byes

⌒

The next morning, Mrs. Darling walked into her children's bedroom and there they were, her babies, sound asleep as though they had never left.

For a moment she thought she must have imagined them leaving in the first place. If it were not for Mr. Darling asleep in his kennel, she wouldn't have been sure.

Of course, the children were only pretending to sleep. Unable to stand the suspense any longer,

they leaped from their beds, screaming, and ran to hug and kiss their mother.

At the commotion, Mr. Darling crawled sleepily out of his kennel. Nana came running into the room as well.

Outside, watching the Darling family reunion from a nearby tree, a little boy named Peter Pan shed a tear. He would never know such happiness, he thought.

The other lost boys were a different story. Wendy had hidden them downstairs, but she summoned them now. She made them stand in a row in front of her mother. She wished they were not all still wearing their pirates' clothes.

"Please take us in," the little pirates begged.

"We don't eat a lot," Nibs said.

"Of course we will have you!" Mrs. Darling cried at once, but Mr. Darling frowned.

"It's an awful lot of boys," he said.

Really, he just wished Mrs. Darling had not answered without asking him. "I just wish people wouldn't treat me like a nobody in my own house," he explained.

"We don't think you are a nobody!" Tootles cried, and the others all agreed.

"You are everything to me," Mrs. Darling whispered to him.

Happy, Mr. Darling said he supposed they could make room, somehow.

As for Peter, he was still outside, lingering. Wendy saw him and walked over to the window.

"Oh, hello," he said casually, as if running into Wendy were a mere coincidence.

"Peter," Wendy said. "Please come inside. My parents will adopt you, too."

Mrs. Darling came over and stood behind her daughter. "It's true," she said.

"You would send me to school and expect me to grow up!" Peter accused. "Deny it!"

But Mrs. Darling couldn't.

"I knew it," Peter cried. "Keep back, madam. No one is going to catch me and make me be a man. I'm going back to Neverland."

"But I'll miss you so much," Wendy said. "I brought back the boys. Perhaps that's enough. Maybe I should go back with you."

Wendy turned to look at her mother.

"Oh, no," Mrs. Darling said quickly.

"But he needs a mother."

"So do you, sweetheart."

Mrs. Darling could see that her decision pained Wendy and Peter, and so she agreed that Wendy could return to Neverland for one week a year to help Peter with the spring cleaning.

Peter was happy with this. He had no sense of time, anyway. He bade Wendy good-bye and said that he would be back in the spring.

The boys went to school. They learned many things but, eventually, they forgot how to fly. They said it was because they were not practicing, but in truth it seemed that they no longer believed. And besides, they no longer had fairy dust to help them. Michael held on to his belief far longer than the others. And Peter did come back, as he'd promised, at the first sign of spring.

Wendy had grown up since he'd seen her last, and she was worried he would notice. He didn't. As usual, he thought and talked mainly about himself. She had been looking forward to reliving old adventures, but Peter had had so many new ones since theirs, he didn't even remember them.

"Who is Captain Hook?" he asked.

"You don't remember killing him and saving all of our lives?"

"I forget them when they are gone," Peter replied.

The next spring, Wendy waited, but Peter never came.

"Maybe he's sick," Michael said. "Maybe we just imagined him."

Wendy cried at that. Could it be?

But the following year, Peter came as planned. He didn't even seem to realize he had missed a year. And that was the last time a girl named Wendy ever saw a boy named Peter Pan.

$\sim$

Years later, when Wendy was married and living in the house she had grown up in, and all of the lost boys were men, she had a little girl named Jane, who loved to ask questions about Peter.

Some days, Wendy could barely remember him—she had already forgotten many details—

and was glad to tell someone about him before she forgot him entirely.

"I know all about him, Mama," Jane said.

Wendy looked up, startled. "You do?" she asked.

"I know him, too," Jane said.

Of course she did, Wendy realized, smiling sadly. All children did.

One day, Wendy was sitting on Jane's bed. She had just finished putting Jane to sleep when Peter flew in through the open window and dropped onto the floor. He was the same as ever.

"Hello, Wendy," he said, as though no time had passed. "Where are John and Michael?"

He looked down at Jane. "Who's that, asleep?"

"Peter," Wendy said, gently. "That's Jane, my daughter. You two have already met in her dreams, if I'm not mistaken?"

Peter wouldn't meet her eyes. He didn't want to admit that Wendy was grown up.

"I don't know what you're talking about," he said firmly. "It's time for spring cleaning, and you promised to come."

"I can't," Wendy said. "I don't remember how to fly."

"I'll teach you again."

Peter seemed about to cry, so Wendy stood up to hug him. But when she did, she loomed so tall above him—obviously a grown-up—that his eyes opened wide in alarm and he gasped.

"It's true, Peter," she said. "I'm grown."

"No! You promised!"

"I couldn't help it," she said. "I'm married now, and a mother."

Peter started to cry, so Wendy went downstairs to get him some warm milk. While she was gone, his sobs woke Jane. She knew at once who the boy was. By the time Wendy returned, Peter was once again laughing, and Jane was flying around the room with him, giggling.

"He needs a mother, Mama," Jane said.

"I know," Wendy said sadly.

Peter pulled Jane over to the window with him, and she went willingly.

"Oh, no," Wendy said, moving between them, just as her own mother once had.

"Just for spring cleaning?" Jane begged.

Wendy shut her eyes.

"All right," she whispered. And—just as Jane would with her own daughter, and Jane's daughter would with her own daughter after that— Wendy watched her baby fly into the sky and off to Neverland until she was as small as the smallest star.

Then, turning from the window, she whispered, "Good night," to Peter, and to Jane, and to you.

What Do *You* Think?
Questions for Discussion

ᴄᴏ

Have you ever been around a toddler who keeps asking the question "Why?" all the time? Does your teacher call on you in class with questions from your homework? Do your parents ask you questions about your day at the dinner table? We are always surrounded by questions that need a specific response. But is it possible to have a question with no right answer?

The following questions are about the book you just read. But this is not a quiz! They are designed to help you look at the people, places, and events in the story from different angles. These questions do not have specific answers. Instead, they might make you think of the story in a completely new way.

Think carefully about each question and enjoy discovering more about this classic story.

1. Why is it so important to Mr. Darling that his family have a nanny? Is this a good reason? Have you ever wanted what someone else had?

2. What do John, Michael, and Wendy's Neverlands look like? What might you find in your Neverland?

3. Why do the stars decide to help Peter? Have you ever done something for fun that ended up upsetting someone else?

4. Peter tells Wendy that no one ever sends him letters. How do you think this makes him feel? Who do you exchange letters with?

5. Peter tells the children that in order to fly,

they need to think happy thoughts. What would you think about?

6. Just before the children leave the nursery, Wendy has second thoughts about how risky flying off would be. What is the riskiest thing you've ever done?

7. Peter's life is full of adventures. Which of these was your favorite? Have you ever had an adventure?

8. What do the children pretend they are eating when they sit down for their imaginary dinner? If you could eat anything for dinner, what would it be?

9. Wendy tells Peter that Curly has his nose, and Peter responds that Michael takes after her. What features do you get from each of *your* parents?

10. Why does Peter hate Wendy's bedtime story? What is your least favorite story? Your favorite?

Afterword

By Arthur Pober, EdD

⟨∞⟩

First impressions are important.

Whether we are meeting new people, going to new places, or picking up a book unknown to us, first impressions count for a lot. They can lead to warm, lasting memories or can make us shy away from any future encounters.

Can you recall your own first impressions and earliest memories of reading the classics?

Do you remember wading through pages and pages of text to prepare for an exam? Or were you the child who hid under the blanket to read with a flashlight, joining forces with Robin Hood to save Maid Marian? Do you remember only how long it took you to read a lengthy novel such as Little Women? Or did you become best friends with the March sisters?

Even for a gifted young reader, getting through long chapters with dense language can easily become overwhelming and can obscure the richness of the story and its characters. Reading an abridged, newly crafted version of a classic novel can be the gentle introduction a child needs to explore the characters and storyline without the frustration of difficult vocabulary and complex themes.

Reading an abridged version of a classic novel gives the young reader a sense of independence and the satisfaction of finishing a "grown-up" book. And when a child is engaged with and inspired by a classic story, the tone is set for further exploration of the story's themes, characters, history, and details. As a child's reading skills advance, the desire to tackle the original, unabridged version of the story will naturally emerge.

If made accessible to young readers, these stories can become invaluable tools for understanding themselves in the context of their families and social environments. This is why the Classic Starts series includes questions that stimulate discussion regarding the impact and social relevance of the characters and stories today. These questions can foster lively conversations between children and their parents or teachers. When we look at the issues, values, and standards of past times in terms of how we live now, we can appreciate literature's classic tales in a very personal and engaging way.

Share your love of reading the classics with a young child, and introduce an imaginary world real enough to last a lifetime.

Dr. Arthur Pober, EdD

Dr. Arthur Pober has spent more than twenty years in the fields of early childhood and gifted education. He is the former principal of one of the world's oldest laboratory schools for gifted youngsters, Hunter College Elementary School, and former Director of Magnet Schools for the Gifted and Talented for more than 25,000 youngsters in New York City.

Dr. Pober is a recognized authority in the areas of media and child protection and is currently the U.S. representative to the European Institute for the Media and European Advertising Standards Alliance.

Explore these wonderful stories in our
Classic Starts™ library.